THE ESCAPE OF MARVIN THE APE

THE ESCAPE OF MARVIN THE APE

by **CARALYN** and **MARK BUEHNER**

PUFFIN BOOKS

It was feeding time, and when the zookeeper wasn't looking, Marvin...

slipped out.

The zookeeper couldn't find Marvin anywhere.

Neither could the police.

Feeling rather hungry, Marvin stopped for a bite.
"Ah, the Jungle Fruit Platter," said the waiter.
"An excellent choice!"

There was a wonderful park nearby. Marvin loved to swing.

At the museum Marvin was delighted to find
a painting done by his Uncle Hairy.

The movie mesmerized Marvin.

Marvin fit right in at the toy store.

Marvin loved the ferry. The sea spray was exhilarating!

Marvin found a lot of places to climb.

At a ball game Marvin
caught a pop-up foul.

Marvin was perfectly content with his new life.

Meanwhile, back at the zoo, it was feeding time and while the zookeeper's head was turned, Helvetica…

dashed out!

To Heidi, Grant, and Sarah
C.B. and M.B.

PUFFIN BOOKS
Published by the Penguin Group
Penguin Putnam Books for Young Readers, 345 Hudson Street, New York, New York 10014, U.S.A.
Penguin Books Ltd, 27 Wrights Lane, London W8 5TZ, England
Penguin Books Canada Ltd, 10 Alcorn Avenue, Toronto, Ontario, Canada M4V 3B2

First published in the United States of America by Dial Books for Young Readers, a division of Penguin Books USA Inc., 1992
Published by Puffin Books, a member of Penguin Putnam Books for Young Readers, 1999

17 19 20 18

THE LIBRARY OF CONGRESS HAS CATALOGED THE DIAL EDITION AS FOLLOWS:
Buehner, Caralyn.
The escape of Marvin the ape / by Caralyn and Mark Buehner;
pictures by Mark Buehner.—1st ed.
p.   cm.
Summary: Marvin the ape slips out of the zoo and finds he likes it
on the outside, where he easily blends into city lifestyles.
ISBN 0-8037-1123-9.—ISBN 0-8037-1124-7 (lib. bdg.)
[1. Apes—Fiction. 2. City and town life—Fiction.] I. Buehner, Mark. II. Title.
PZ7.B884Es 1992 [E]—dc20 91-10795 CIP AC

Puffin Books ISBN 978-0-14-056503-4

Printed in China